The Ways I Help

I Help at Grandpa's House

Beatrice Mortmain

illustrated by
Aurora Aguilera

PowerKiDS press.

New York

Published in 2018 by The Rosen Publishing Group, Inc.
29 East 21st Street, New York, NY 10010

First Edition

Managing Editor: Nathalie Beullens-Maoui
Editor, English: Theresa Morlock
Book Design: Raúl Rodriguez
Illustrator: Aurora Aguilera

Cataloging-in-Publication Data

Names: Mortmain, Beatrice.
Title: I help at grandpa's house / Beatrice Mortmain.
Description: New York : PowerKids Press, 2018. | Series: The ways I help | Includes index.
Identifiers: ISBN 9781508156772 (pbk.) | ISBN 9781508157373 (library bound) | ISBN 9781538320358 (6 pack)
Subjects: LCSH: Grandfathers–Juvenile fiction. | Helping behavior–Juvenile fiction.
Classification: LCC PZ7.M678 Ihe 2018 | DDC [E]–dc23

Manufactured in the United States of America

CPSIA Compliance Information: Batch #BS17PK: For further information contact Rosen Publishing, New York, New York at 1-800-237-9932

Contents

My grandpa's house
is next to mine.

I like to visit him every day.

Grandpa has a dog named Rufus.
Rufus and Grandpa are both very old.

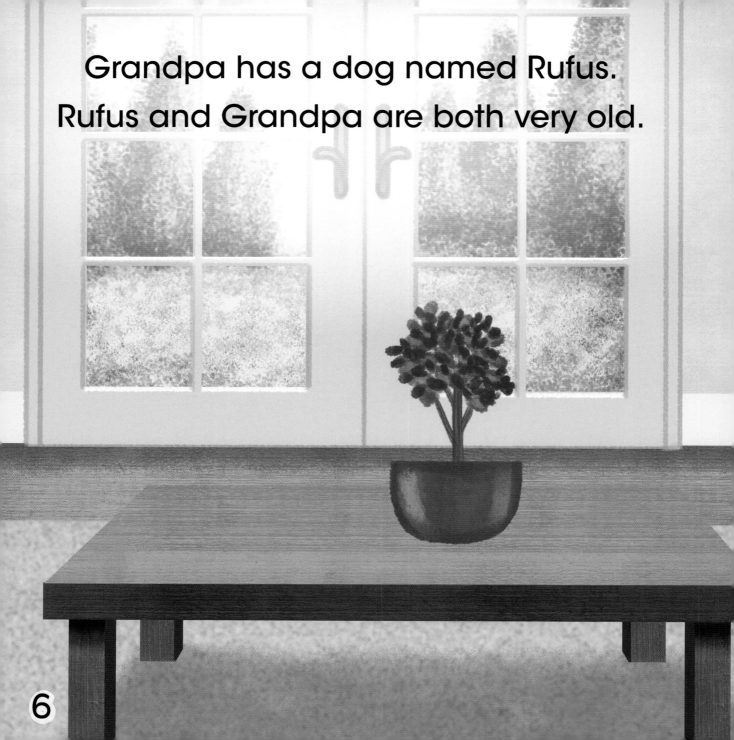

7

Grandpa asks me to read him the newspaper. I like to use silly voices.

9

Grandpa asks if I'd like a snack.
We make a plate of
carrot sticks and celery.

Sometimes Grandpa's knees are sore.
I help Grandpa by taking Rufus for a walk.

Grandpa asks me to help him do the dishes. He washes the dishes and I dry them and put them away.

14

15

Grandpa likes to do puzzles.

16

We put a puzzle together
piece by piece.

When the puzzle is finished
we clean up the living room.

I sweep the kitchen.

Grandpa looks sleepy. He wants to take a nap.

I get him his slippers.

It's time for me to go home
for today. Helping my
Grandpa makes me
feel proud.

23

Words to Know

newspaper

puzzle

slippers

Index